For Mum and Dad, Jeff, Deba, and my Wadjigany family
— may Brother Moon forever guide your way.
MMY

For my Pa, and in memory of Popsy Dazzler.
SF

Brother Moon

MAREE McCARTHY YOELU

illustrated by

SAMANTHA FRY

Great-Grandpa Liman lives by the sea.
There are no lights — just stars
as far as the eye can see.

When the sun goes down,
we sit by the fire
and listen to the waves.

'Let me tell you a story
about my brother,'
says Great-Grandpa.

'Who is your brother?' I ask.

'Open your eyes and ears, Hippy-boy.
By the end of my story, you will
know my brother.'

'My brother is wise and never grows old. As the sun disappears beyond the horizon, my brother stops by. He knows that I am wary of the darkness.'

‘At night, when it is cool, I hunt for my tucker.

I stay alert for the boars and buffalos that wander freely here.

My brother shows me the way, and my fears disappear.’

'The ocean is my shop, but there are dangers in the water.

I call on my brother to shine his light, and I see the eyes of crocodiles.'

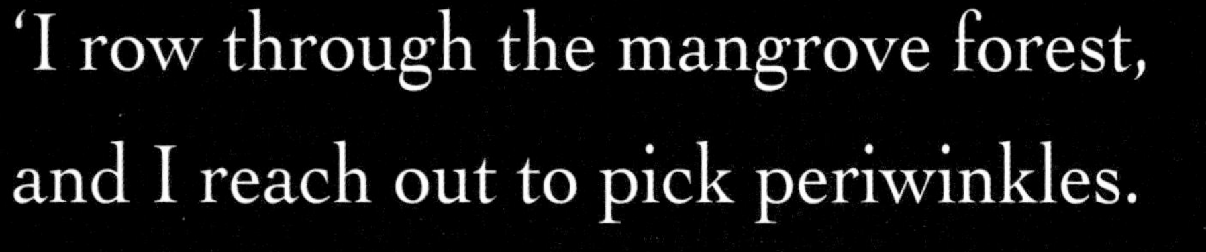

'I row through the mangrove forest,
and I reach out to pick periwinkles.

My brother peers through the branches.'

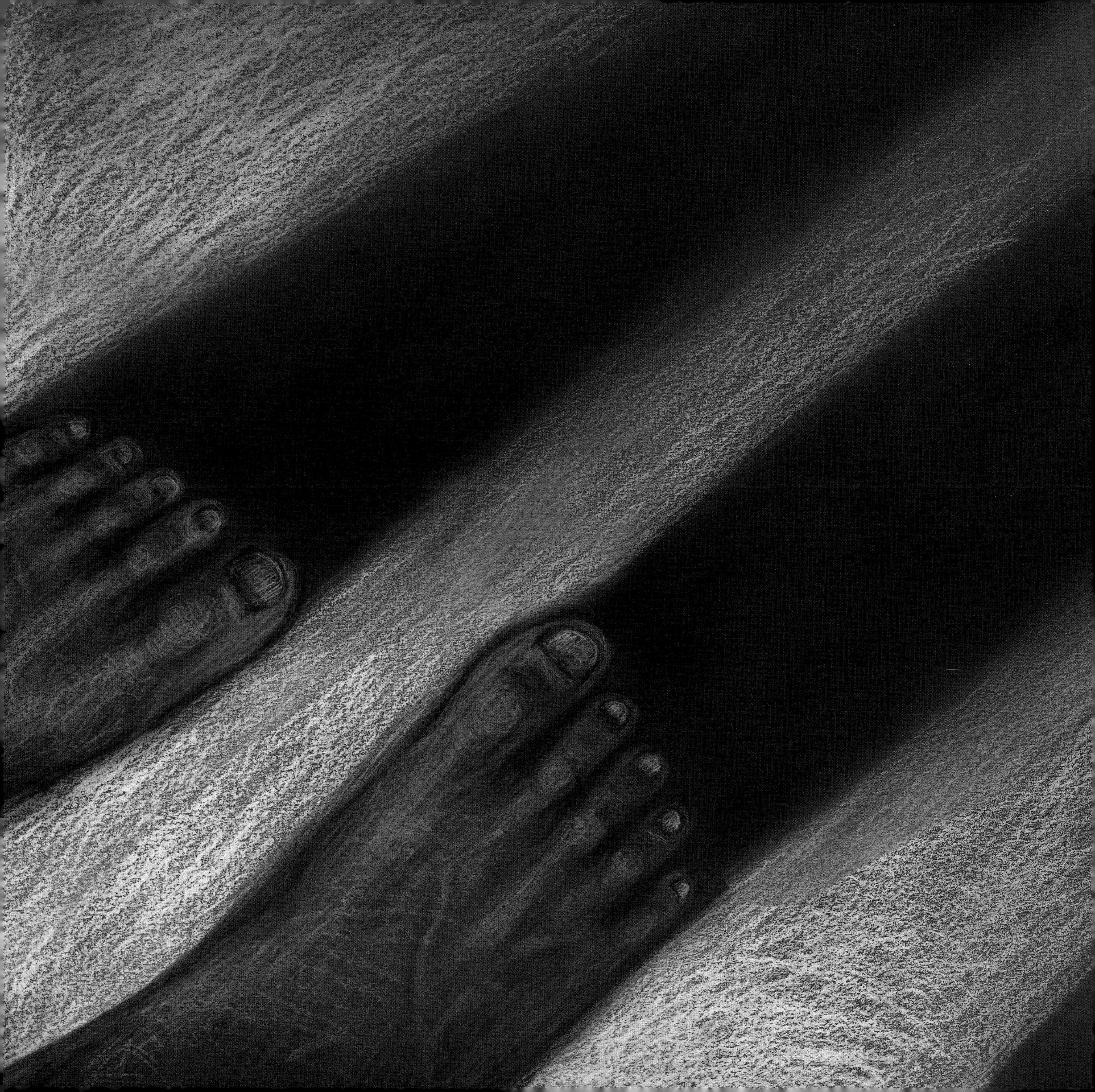

‘Sometimes, I hear slithering noises in my shack.
I try not to be scared when a snake comes looking for food.

My brother turns up when I need him the most.’

'My brother can be big and bold.
Even when he is half here, he is my brother and
he is always with me.

He breathes in the air and the beauty around him.

He changes shape. He gets round and full –
– until finally he bursts, scattering his glow across
the earth's shadows.

Who is my brother, Hippy-boy?'
asks Great-Grandpa.

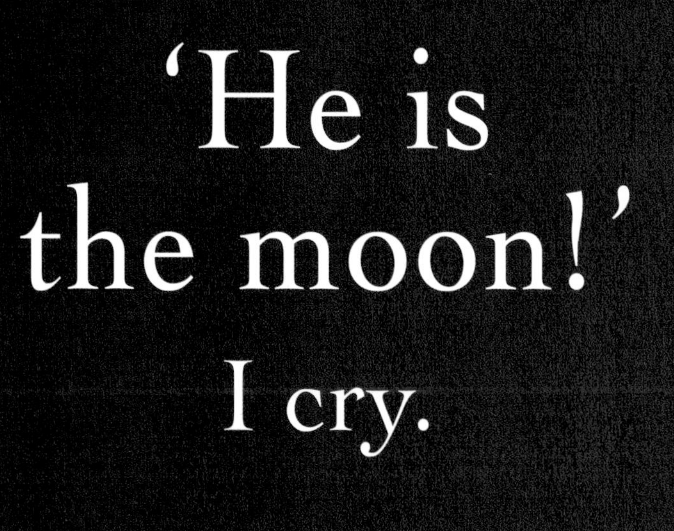

'He is
the moon!'
I cry.

'Yes,' says Great-Grandpa.
'Near or far, old or new,
his glow is always brightest
in the dark.

He is my brother –
the moon.'

I fall asleep under the night sky.
Just Brother Moon and me,
and Great-Grandpa Liman.

LIMAN (HARRY MORGAN) was a respected Wadjigany man — a leader amongst his people and the community.

Liman was born at Manjimamany (Point Blaze) in the Northern Territory in 1916.

He was a canoe maker, hunter, community mediator and a family man, who lived off the land and travelled the seas. Liman spoke Batjamalh, his first language, and other languages from the Daly River area.

Liman was also a wonderful storyteller. He told the story of Brother Moon to Hippy (Heath Wilson), his great-grandson, when Hippy first visited Wadjigany country as a small boy.

Hippy, a young Wadjigany and Tyemirri man, still returns to Wadjigany country to hunt and fish, and spend time with family.

MAREE MCCARTHY YOELU is a Wadjigany woman, from the western Wagait region in the Northern Territory. She grew up in Daly River and now lives in Darwin where she works in radio. Liman is Maree's grandfather. She writes to keep his stories and the Batjamalh language alive for generations to come. This is her first book.

SAMANTHA FRY is descended from the Dagiman people of the Katherine region in the Northern Territory. As a child she lived in communities across the Top End. Samantha is an accomplished artist and designer living in Darwin. She is the illustrator of the celebrated children's book *Alfred's War* (Magabala Books 2018).

First published 2020, reprinted 2022, 2024 and 2025
Magabala Books Aboriginal Corporation, Broome, Western Australia
W: www.magabala.com E: sales@magabala.com

Magabala Books receives financial assistance from the Commonwealth Government through Creative Australia, its arts advisory body. The State of Western Australia has made an investment in this project through the Department of Local Government, Sport and Cultural Industries.

Magabala Books is Australia's only independent Aboriginal and Torres Strait Islander publishing house. Magabala Books acknowledges the Traditional Owners of the Country on which we live and work. We recognise the unbroken connection to traditional lands, waters and cultures. Through what we publish, we honour all our Elders, peoples and stories, past, present and future.

Colour reproduction by Splitting Image Colour Studio Pty Ltd

Printed in China by Toppan Leefung Printing Ltd

The illustrations in this book were drawn with coloured pencil on coloured paper.

ISBN 978 1 925936 82 7